The House in the Night

For Tom, Nicholas, and Benjamin
—my family
—S.M.S.

For my girls
—B.K.

Text copyright © 2008 by Susan Marie Swanson
Illustrations copyright © 2008 by Beth Krommes

The text of this book is set in Cronos Pro Semibold Display.
The illustrations are scratchboard and watercolor.
Book design by Carol Goldenberg

Library of Congress Cataloging-in-Publication Data

Swanson, Susan Marie.
The house in the night / written by Susan Marie Swanson and illustrated by Beth Krommes.
p. cm.
Summary: Illustrations and easy-to-read text explore the light that makes a house in the night a home filled with light.
ISBN-13: 978-0-618-86244-3 (hardcover)
ISBN-10: 0-618-86244-7 (hardcover)
[1. Dwellings—Fiction. 2. Light—Fiction. 3. Night—Fiction.] I. Krommes, Beth, ill. II. Title.
PZ7.S97255Hou 2008
[E]—dc22
2007012921

Printed in Singapore
TWP 10 9 8 7 6 5 4 3 2

The House in the Night

Written by
SUSAN MARIE SWANSON

Pictures by
BETH KROMMES

HOUGHTON MIFFLIN COMPANY ❧ BOSTON 2008

Here is the key
to the house.

In the house
burns a light.

In that light
rests a bed.

On that bed
waits a book.

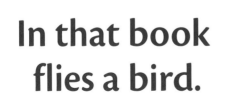

In that book
flies a bird.

**all about
the starry dark.**

Through the dark
glows the moon.

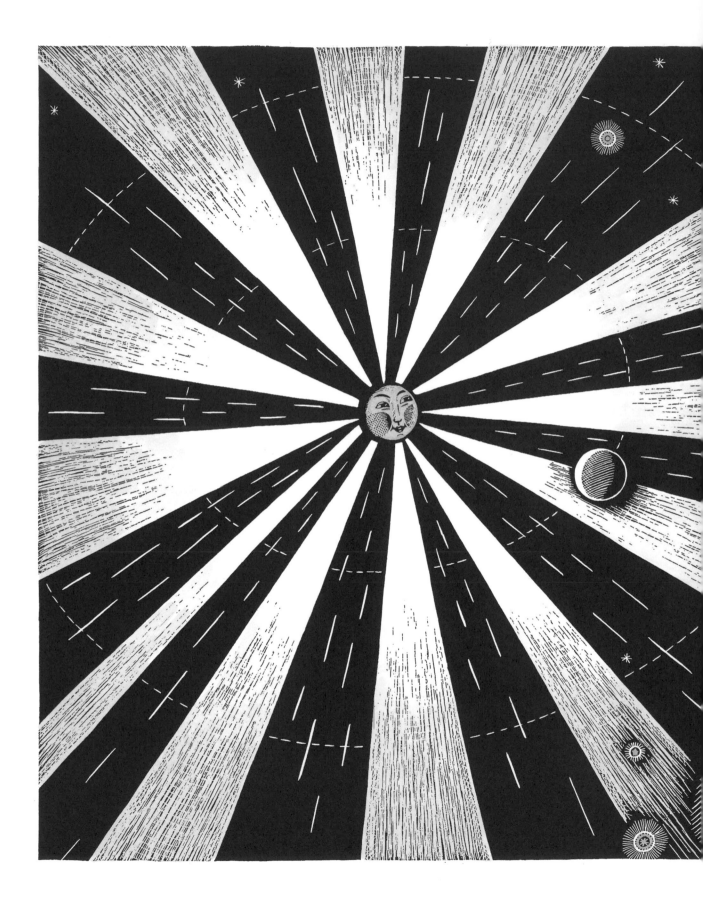

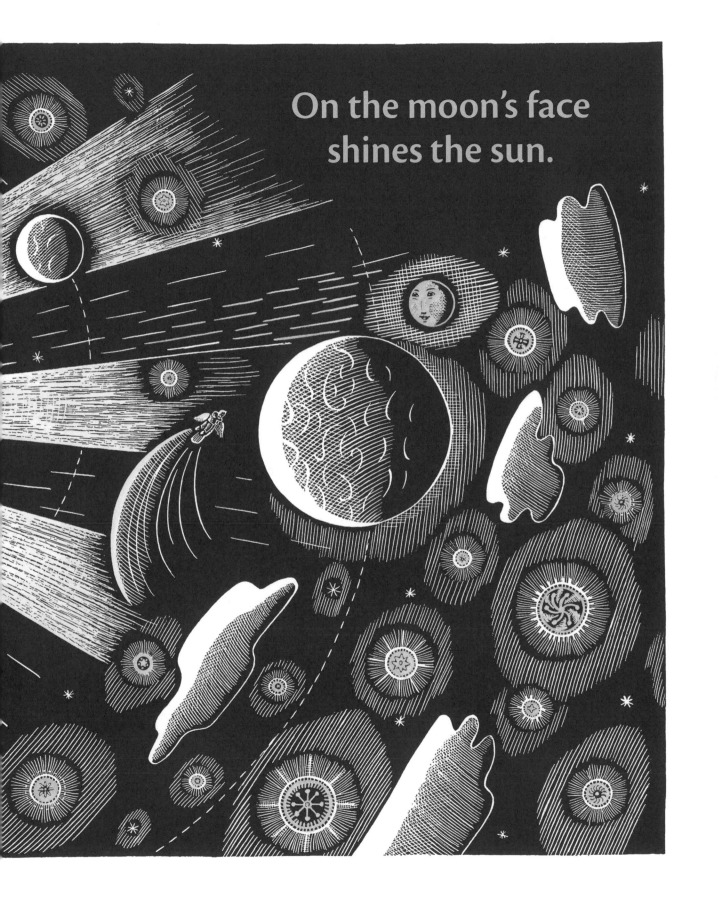

On the moon's face
shines the sun.

Sun in the moon,

moon in the dark,

dark in the song,

song in the bird,

bird in the book,

book on the bed,

bed in the light,

light in the house.

Here is the
key to
the house,

the house
in the night,

a home
full of light.

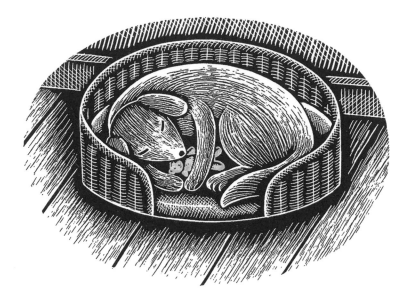

Author's Note

In *The Oxford Nursery Rhyme Book*, first published in 1955, Iona and Peter Opie collected nursery rhymes handed down over many years, including one that begins, "This is the key of the kingdom: / In that kingdom is a city, / In that city is a town, / In that town there is a street . . ." Like other traditional poems with cumulative patterns, such as "Hush, little baby, don't say a word" and "This is the house that Jack built," "This is the key of the kingdom" has long been one of my favorites, and it inspired the pattern of this picture book.